love, and other love

love, and other love

caleb graves

love, and other love © 2024 Caleb Graves

All rights reserved

Printed in the United States of America

No part of this book may be used or reproduced in any form or by any means without permission, except in the brief case of quotations for critical reviews.

First printing 2024

ISBN 979-8-218-45780-8

Cover art copyright 2024 © Caleb Graves

www.calebgwrites.com

for mom, whose love is the kind that never ends

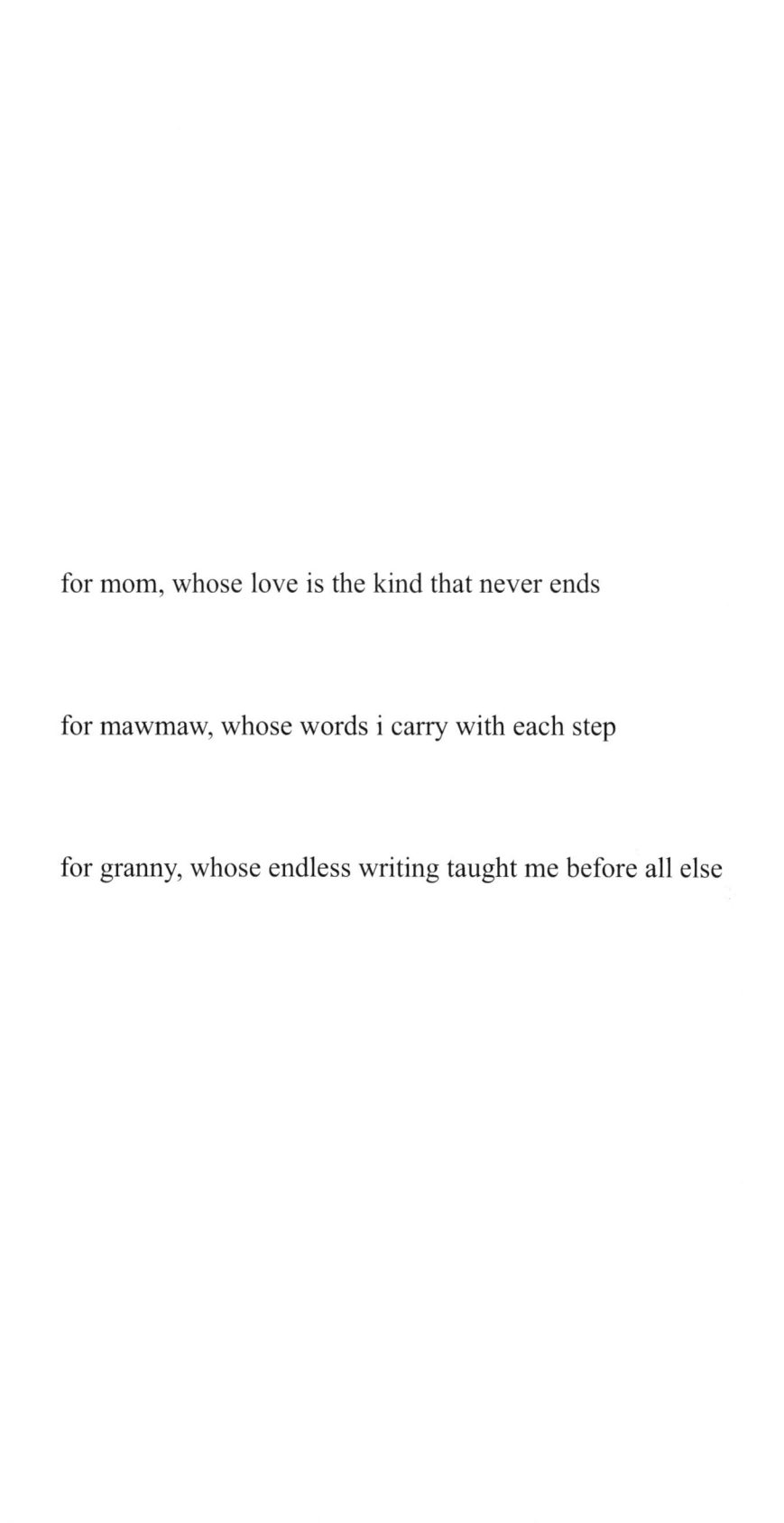

for mawmaw, whose words i carry with each step

for granny, whose endless writing taught me before all else

CONTENTS

love   1

I.

the beginning   5
rules   7
night   9
new world   11
family   12
young   13

II.

school   17
heavy   18
code   19
message boards   20
not uncharted   22
crash   23
honesty pains   25
losing your best friend to love   27
playlist   29
over   30
the hard part   32
flight   33

III.

drought   37

chase	38
austin	39

IV.

a real good lie	43
run	44
a bus to galway	45
twenties	46
the kitchen	47
out loud	48
stretched across miles	49
leftovers	50
on to the next test	51
overlap	52
walking the beach at night	54
alone in paris on valentine's day	55
divorce	57
selective observation	58
bad trip	60
gone	61
alone	62
playing games	63
while we sleep	65
australia	66
acting	67
texting	69
turn around	70

first sight	72
learning something new	74
fighting with indifference	75
wedding bells	76
happy birthday	78
friday nights	80
just friends	82
swimming back	83
mirror image	85
waiting game	86
the chase	87

V.

starting over	91
film	92
it's early	94
december	95
stars	96
history	98
open eyes	100
i hate the internet	102
mornings	104
so many things	105
italian food	106
research	108
vacation	109
spoken in the dark	111

when you hold my hand	114
different	115
work	116
missing out	117
afraid	119

VI.

vindicated	123
left behind	124
tragedies	126
beer cans in a bar	127
where are the doctors	130
wednesday	131
new things	132
sleeping	133
twist	135
upside	137
ghost runner	138
museum date	139
and again	140
hints	141
judgment	142
december again	144
aftertaste	146

VII.

the portrait	149

old ways	150
swim	151
tuesday	152
code braker	153
loving this city	154
just go	156
know	157
other things	158
the flood	159
VIII.	
real	165
move on	166
change	167
Acknowledgments	169
About the Author	171

<u>love</u>

you'll just... know.

the answer
from every parent and every movie and
every song should you ever decide to ask
what is love?

no other question or query
escapes scrutiny like that.
not a shoe with laces.
not a driving test.
not a twenty-seven piece
furniture set scattered across your living room floor.

if this answer is a waving white flag
because the thing is too complicated,
too twisted in the tree's roots
deep underground,
then we should confess.
i am skeptical of such a plain response
that thrives on hopeful sighs.
i have found love is never so simple.

there is love they tell you about.
there is love you hope for.
there is love as you first find it.
and there is other love.
and still other, *other* love.

and i am not sure which is best.

if any of them.

I.

<u>the beginning</u>

we are doomed from birth.

in the first few moments
when we are blind,
cold, cradled by latexed hands,
when we gasp for breath
under foggy fluorescence,
our ears,
as tiny as they are,
as new as they are,
as innocent as they are,
sense foreign vibrations.

but those first few words,
hum like a symphony
in our tiny beating heart.
in those first few phrases,
often repeated,
sometimes cried,
no matter the circumstances
of what led a mother to this moment,
are three simple words.

those words will haunt us forever.

we will chase their meaning,
yearning for something
akin to the warm safety
nesting deep in our souls
in those first moments.

we are birthed explorers,

ready to search the planet
from the moment the words pass
over a mother's lips—

i love you

<u>rules</u>

stop!
she whisper screamed at me
inside the metal tunnel
where we hid.
other kindergarteners ran
laughing and playing,
but we were too busy growing up
in our playground silo.

why?
i asked.

there are rules.

what are the rules?

it was my first time.
i didn't know the rules.
i didn't even know there were rules.

before you can kiss me,
you have to say it.

say what?

you know what!
stop being a stupid boy!

i didn't think i was stupid.
i came to kindergarten
already reading.

before you can kiss me,
you have to say
you love me.

that's it?
i almost laughed
i just have to say that?

she nodded.
i shrugged.

okay.
i love you.

she smiled.
okay you can kiss me now.

and so i kissed her.
the moment was so brief
i could not be sure it even happened
but for the new sound of lips meeting
and the lingering taste of cherry.

then i opened my eyes
to a disgusted face.

yuck!

she twisted around,
scrambled on hands and knees
out of the tunnel,
and ran.

we never spoke again.

<u>night</u>

as a boy,
i thought love was
hidden in the dark.

the unrelenting sun
being too much,
it sought the solace of night,
riding cool breezes
while the world slumbered,
barely visible beneath the
twinkling light of stars.

i had proof.
i watched aladdin and jasmine
find it time after time
on that old VHS tape
that told the tale of agrabah.

before they tumbled through
an endless diamond sky,
everything got in the way:
food,
money,
family,
status,
power,
pride,
a loud talking bird.

but high above the city,
away from all else,
with nothing but each other,

a little magic,
in the dead of night,
they found the rarest thing.

so at five years old
i wanted to fly.

<u>new world</u>

when i was six,
my parents divorced.

so i stopped hearing real people
say i love you for a long time,
unless they were bound by blood.

magic carpets
sunk to the ground.

gravity was stronger.

<u>family</u>

years turned over
with me thinking
love only mattered
in the moments
where a family still breathed.

love was pancakes like
mawmaw made them
at the table together.

love was going to soccer games
on saturday mornings.
love was us all opening
our first gift on christmas eve.

love was mom driving
the three of us to school,
eating breakfast in the car
almost late again,
the four of us together
sharing the same air.

<u>young</u>

i left those early years
with no real idea
of what love is supposed to be.

maybe that is okay.
a pre-teen boy
not burdened with
an endless puzzle
where too many pieces
look the same.

after all,
the only example
that stuck with me
of kids falling in love
was a movie where a boy dies
from a bee allergy.
i guess i learned
even that young
love is unexpectedly
interrupted.

II.

school

they traded boyfriends and girlfriends
like pokémon cards.
passing love letters in algebra
and at half-open lockers,
signing off with love
on flip phones
before the internet
blended with oxygen.

i was averse to it,
or never got picked anyway,
or was too busy anyway,
always a test to study for,
so i settled for books.

i read about a wizard
burned with a bolt of lightning,
alive thanks to love.
he exhaled that love
onto friends who never
saw him as an outcast.

i worked whatever
earthly enchantments i could
to find something like that,
a friend who would follow
you into the dark.
i was already scared
of haunted houses
and the clowns
that called them home.

heavy

brown hair and
brown eyes,
both of us.
we talked by phone
every night.

once when saying bye,
you said it to me,
quickly and nervously,
and my heart skipped a beat,
and i said it back.

after we hung up
my body felt heavier,
gaining weight i would never shed.
i had bitten the apple,
burned with something new,
forced from quiet gardens
that would welcome me no more,
cast into barren lands with no guide,
not even a broken path to follow.

<u>code</u>

even though our families
were not warring to stage us
across two distant stars,
we lived by a code.
telephone calls and
we were surrounded.
it's time to go to bed,
or dinner is ready,
or i need to use the phone now.
we would pause,
i would smile big
and coyly say
cool.

and you would say it back.
everyday slang to keep
the string invisible to spectators
who will continue to think
we are doing just fine.

a code for only us,
as if love needed to be
more cryptic.

message boards

it never felt weird
to make friends online.
i connected with people
based on words they wrote
and ideas we shared.
loving the same books,
hating the same characters,
hoping to see the same
parts of the world someday,
loving halloween,
sharing a sense of humor,
and correctly using
an oxford comma.

but it branched into weird
when people fell
in love
online.
head over heels for someone
you can only reach
if the dial-up connection
does not falter?
it could not be real.

so i took on the role of skeptic,
rolling my eyes and
heckling digital romance,
even as i formed friendships
in the same way,
bonds i still have today.

now,
i wonder,
which i doubted more:
the power of words?
or the heart's knack
for finding a reason to beat
by any means possible?

<u>not uncharted</u>

euphoria was not
enough to get me
around the track.
my body was built
for running long distances.
i sought sources of stamina,
counting on love that flows
from springs not tainted by romance
that could keep me running for years.
so sure i was wise to
drink from waters
that knew their path,
simple streams that may
twist and turn and wind
this way and that,
but whose course i knew
with my own heart,
those that never veered far
even as i took my own
steps into the distance.

<u>crash</u>

the terror of losing
the loves that are
meant to last forever,
blood-bound,
starring roles
in every memory.

the day is average,
later you will recall
things you always forget.
the cereal for breakfast,
dropping the spoon
on the way to the sink,
three cars at the stop sign
when you pulled up,
hearing birds before anything
when you open the door.

at work,
a phone call,
an accident,
speeding to the hospital,
sprinting inside,
you on a hospital bed,
leg wrapped up,
eyes shut,
body still.
losing control of my own
and crashing to the floor.

at eighteen
my life was nearly ripped apart,

i learned how you can be destroyed
because of what you love.

<u>honesty pains</u>

you were the first.

the first person
to say you love me
and actually mean it.
and i do not even think
i need to qualify it by saying
as much as a teenager
thinks they love someone.

you really loved me.
and that made me
want to love you, too.
i really wanted to.

i wanted to whisper
it back to you
that very first time.
i wanted to stand outside
in hot summer pouring rain,
drenched clothes and moppy hair,
shout it,
then kiss you long and hard
like there were
cameras and lights
pointed only on us
to tell the greatest love story.
if i just would have said it,
i know there was a
happy ending waiting
for us to redeem.

but i could not meet you there,
and it killed me.
and i am sorry still.

losing your best friend to love

i don't know if i was
such a rigid rational thinker
before we became friends,
or if that's how you were
and i wanted to emulate you.
but at some point
we both agreed that
love was a choice,
not a feeling,
and that everyone else
was silly and immature.

but then you found love,
so you said.
and it was the start
of us falling apart.
i know now that
friends simply fall apart,
but then i only tasted
the bitterness of betrayal,
you, now an oathbreaker,
carelessly airborne,
pulled by the thin feeble tail
of a flimsy kite.

did you not ever fear
the sun would ignite
those temporary wings?

i buried my feet,
miles and miles underground,
living there,

calling myself disciplined,
wearing a ribbon in the darkness,
looking past the spite that
crawled in the dirt
between my fingers and toes.

playlist

for graduation,
i gave you a gift.
a mix CD of our favorite songs.
back when music
was not so available
and there was art
in reorganizing melody
into a physical home.

a custom print label
stuck to the top,
a picture of us
barely smiling,
but very happy.

i almost made a copy
for myself.
i wonder how it would
sound now.

<u>over</u>

we did not have
friendship bracelets
or framed photos of each other.
they say boys should not do that.

we had inside jokes,
and punk bands,
and disdain for school
even though we were both good at it,
and plans to go to college together
until i learned we didn't after all.

it took a very long time
to feel that kind of loss again.
the sudden emptiness
that swallows every
ticking second,
the irregular cycling
through stages of grief
with new stops along the way,
ones i had never been taught,
like indifference to the world
and madness.

but on the other side,
when the smoke left my eyes
i saw it true at last—
the painting that
had hung on my walls
for far too long,
surviving many fires,
finally unraveled.

the spell was broken.
i watched the portrait
crack, crumble, and fade,
and you did, too.

the hard part

we both cried.
sitting in my red pontiac
at the city park.

i think you thought
we would be forever.

it broke me to break you.
i would have done anything
to heal your wounds,
except the one and only thing
that actually would.
because i knew
we were not a song
the stars longed for.

that night,
i felt wise
and heartbroken.
irony's arrow had
struck too true.
a pained heart for confessing
there would never be love.

flight

leaving my hometown,
a village that set
the boundaries of
many universes.
for me,
an endless carousel
where questions
are not allowed.

i fled for college.

it was the beginning
of my great, long love affair
with leaving
and starting over.

III.

drought

college was
cheap thrills,
foggy mornings,
and dollar beers.
love felt forgotten
and extraterrestrial.
why would i search
out something foreign?

i loved no one for four years.
least of all myself.

i drowned in
doubt and insecurity,
only to stand up just in time
to gasp for air,
learning i could touch
in that pool all along.

but instead of
appreciating my height,
i let myself slip again,
i don't remember which
foot gave way first,
sinking down, down…

<u>chase</u>

you turn twenty.
instead of marking
a new decade,
you start counting down
to the next year.
your ID will matter more.
it feeds the addiction
of chasing something
not yet there.
or is it a treatment?
looking deeper
into the sun,
blinding yourself
to the still, fruitless earth
as it rotates again and again,
waiting for an irregular shift.
the poles have not
traded places for almost
a million years.

austin

i knew austin
was temporary.

for all i loved there,
and there was much—
barbecue and
breakfast tacos and
burnt orange saturdays and
bonnell and
barton springs—
i knew the heavy humid air
would come to know me too well.
it would pull at my skin
until i was glued
to the ground,
forcing me to sit
alone with myself
for far longer
than i could bear.

no, i would keep moving,
run away to a place where
the winds do not know my name.

IV.

<u>a real good lie</u>

the problem with love
in this timeline
is the person who shows you
love can be real
is also the person who shows you
love can be a lie.

run

i love to run.

this is not a metaphor.
at least not primarily.

i have found that
nothing clears my mind
quite like the rhythm of
my feet hitting pavement
one-two-three-four
my arms swinging at my sides
one-two-three-four
my lips channeling steady breaths
one-two-three-four.

if i could always
breathe so steady
one, two, th—

<u>a bus to galway</u>

twenty-two
in ireland alone.

a bus from dublin
to galway.
i regret not renting a car
and spending more time
driving the countryside,
marveling at this
beautiful green paradise
that has always oddly felt
foreign and home
simultaneously.

but i took the bus instead.
across the aisle,
she was beautiful.
damp dirty blonde hair,
pale blue eyes
like calm steady waves
under an evening sky.

we made eye contact
a few times,
filling my stomach
with butterflies.
maybe irish butterflies,
if there were butterflies
specific to this emerald isle.

we never spoke.
i can still see her now.

<u>twenties</u>

choose yourself
in your twenties.
that is what
i told myself.
it took me to
new cities and new jobs,
new people and new lives.

how can you choose someone else
when you are always choosing
yourself?

how can you expect someone else
to then choose you?

but if they did...
no.

<u>the kitchen</u>

a beautiful smile,
a confident voice,
and just enough sarcasm
to keep me on my toes.

it has been six months now
and this feels like what
happy might be.
you buy me things
that most people don't
even know that i love.
we cook in the kitchen.
together.
or you cook,
and i watch you
over my wine glass.

i drink wine these days.

i drink wine and
i feel warm.

<u>out loud</u>

hearing them say
i love you
and even though
it was unexpected
and came as a total surprise,
you do not stare back
or stammer.
you make good
on the agreement
between your head
and your heart,
having never decided
on which drew up
the papers first,
and say it back.

you believe yourself.
you believe your own words.

<u>stretched across miles</u>

the mistake of
buying stock
in a long-distance affair.

a terrible year.
doing it all over again.
i demand the same flavor
of chewing gum
and ignore suggestions
for a faster route.

so i only find love
in a room painted
in shades of familiarity.
held constant is me
testing just how far
my heart can stretch
across miles and miles.

if someone would just
smile at me in the coffee shop.

leftovers

radio silence
for four full days.
a new record for us.
scrolling socials to see
your secrets in a
facebook comment thread.
a month ago, maybe more,
i found his hoodie
in your closet.
why would you hold on
to something like that?
texas is usually hot,
and closet space is small.
when i asked,
you got defensive,
but never answered.

i think i preferred the silence.
what breaks the ice
might melt the planet.

<u>on to the next test</u>

studying for a final exam
i told my friend we broke up,
recounted the war's final days,
how i fought with anything
within reach
while you journaled defeat
in different fonts.

my friend looked at me
without a typical
oh i'm so sorry
mournful gaze.
she smiled,
and something else,
was that a smirk?
then said casually
she's young.
she doesn't get how to make
a relationship work.

and then we started studying.
and then i started to forget you.
i was still in my twenties
anyway.

<u>overlap</u>

struggling to open up
to friends more often
thanks to how i crave
to create the impression
that i am strong
and independent
and undeterred
by trivial things
like love.

but partly,
though i can never say it,
or they will be on
the next train out,
is that i cannot trust them.
how can they guide me
if they have not lived
the same moment
themselves?
past experiences do not help.
not with love.
we look back at storied paths
with disdain,
itching for revenge,
or at least a stroke of ink
toward self-preservation.

we can relate to losing a job
or a boss being miserable
because we have all experienced it
and all jobs are awful anyway.
we can talk through

choosing a college or
picking a house or
justifying still driving
a gasoline car even though
the environment is unraveling
all around us every day
but i am just so worried about
getting stuck in the middle of
some road with no
charging station in sight
and i will probably be surrounded by
three gas stations when i do.

the traps we lay for ourselves.

but we cannot
fully and confidently
talk through love with one another.
the internal chemistry
is never mimed for any two people.

so i play
my bitter symphony
to an audience
of one.

walking the beach at night

every night
we walk the beach together,
our new moonlight tradition.
sand nesting between our toes,
salt air tingling my nose,
we walk side by side
but not too close.
in the dark,
only guided by
faint stars and
flicking fluorescent,
i imagine reaching out
for your hand.
we are safe at night.
no outside scrutiny
with a slumbering sun.
we could walk the shore
with fingers interlocked
until we run out of sand.

alone in paris on valentine's day

it's valentine's day
and i wander
the streets of paris
alone.

i stressed to friends
that i did not plan
to go to paris alone
for this ridiculous holiday,
that it was merely coincidence.
just good timing.

still,
the thought crosses my mind
that i somehow led myself to
the city of love
for this occasion.
but i stand at the edge
of the bridge
and throw that thought
as far as i can,
turning before i can see
how the seine
swallows it hole.

i walk with a crepe warming my hand.
i sit in the luxembourg gardens,
bare and nearly empty in winter,
but still somehow beautiful.
i spend hours in d'orsay,
floating among water lilies,
wondering if monet

ever kept count of them,
one for each blossomed love,
or if such precision
trivializes the art.
they all keep floating, anyway.

the best french onion soup
i have ever had.
a table for two
in a busy restaurant,
avoiding eye contact
with those in wait outside.
but maybe they
do not detest me.
the people of paris
are much nicer than
the stories of those
who have never been
might suggest.
these window companions
are romantics, i think,
and so perhaps charmed
by a valentine's dinner alone.

<u>divorce</u>

before you,
everyone else
had two parents who
still loved each other,
at least as far as
the government knows.
and doesn't it know too much?

i always dreaded the moment
i would meet the parents,
a couple who still shared a bed,
a bank account,
maybe a shower now and again.

oh, my parents are divorced.
the reactions were usually
of mild surprise,
like i was a rare species
that never frequented these parts
where two-car garages
are actually used.

but you,
you are the same as me.
we must not walk on eggshells
and act convincingly like
we are not damaged goods
from a broken promise.
you know,
truly know,
what it means
for it to not be my fault.

<u>selective observation</u>

the drinks are strong at this bar
that has taken being trendy
way too far,
a mix of sculptures
and antique phones
holding too much space.
this place does not know
who it wants to be.

but this is your favorite bar in this city,
a city that was once mine,
but not for quite some time.
strange to be a visitor
in what was my first new home.

two guys walk by,
barely-buttoned flannels
rolled up at the elbow.
hands and forearms
bare and ready.
they walk by and eye you.
of course they do.
you are beautiful.
you glow golden,
just like your hair,
with sharp blue eyes
that send electrons
firing in a frenzy of light.
your energy promises
to breathe new life
into anything you touch.

do i tell you that enough?
i don't.
these things i notice
only when strangers are mirrors.
it is unbecoming.
it will be an undoing.

bad trip

you watched me
have a panic attack
halfway across the world.
like almost everything else,
i try to hide my anxious tendencies
in a small drawer of a dresser
that can blend in with any room.
but this time i lost
my contacts and deodorant
and a lot of other replaceable things
in a place far from home.

you saw me at my worst,
when being rational
was a shrunken sweater
that no longer fit,
and thinking clearly
was a rattling wooden bridge
that i may never trust again.

but you did not run.
you took me to a pharmacy
and later rubbed my shoulders.
i was able to fall asleep
so easily that night.

<u>gone</u>

in 2019
my grandma died.
she made me fall in love
with donuts.
she told me i would be handsome
even wearing a paper sack.
she took me to bookstores.
she wrote me cards in college
because she knew
i loved writing
and appreciated when
others did too.

she was the first person i lost
who made me think
you'll never meet the person i marry.

impossible
that someday
i might find love
that could last a lifetime,
but she would never
see what it does to me,
what it does for me.

i want to connect
all of the people
i love together.

we do not have
enough time.

<u>alone</u>

trying to be there for me
when my grandma died
when all i wanted was to be alone
because that was the only thing
that felt real and right
because alone is all i felt
with her gone.

a few weeks later
you said that this
was not working for you
anymore,

you told me
that you told my best friend
that you loved me.

you never told me.

this is a thing
i never want.

<u>playing games</u>

i never much loved board games.
but i thoroughly enjoy
the games i play
in my own mind.

instead of going to therapy,
i map out what that stranger
with a pen and a couch
and a lot more questions than answers
would say when i finally admit
that i am terrified of being left.
they will ask about my father
and if i treat with this terror
because i never felt sure
he loved me,
or i him,
even though we both said it dutifully,
even as we saw each other less and less,
and i will respond,
to the person who profits
on my problems,
that this all sounds
a lot more like answers than questions.

the game turns from twenty questions
to collecting cards,
all the places i can imagine
where i might be left.

a subway stop,
a coffee shop,
a doorstep,

a park bench,
a saturday brunch.

i leave places sometimes
simply because i can.

with another sleeping next to me,
sometimes i wake
in the middle of the night
and move to the couch,
just so i can leave first.

while we sleep

my first time in your new city.
you lead me to brunch
and museums and coffee shops
and street vendors
who have the kindest smiles.

we walk through two different parks,
one small and another not.
there are options here.

at night,
we share your bed,
but only to sleep.
the couch is too small for me.
i wake with your hand
on my stomach.
your eyes are closed.
i feel the pulse in your wrist
thumping against my skin,
sending shockwaves north and south.

i could lie like this for hours.

you rustle,
never waking,
retract your hand,
and turn to face the wall.
i do not fall asleep for
what feels like hours.
when i do,
i dream of two birds
soaring over a purple ocean.

australia

a news story about the dying
great barrier reef,
and i remember falling for you
on that island continent
so far from home.

it is all still there in my head,
watching you look at me,
seeing me from a distance,
taking me all in.
like i was unlike anything
you had ever seen before.
i had never felt a high like that.

i went back home to america
and still tried to talk to you.
but then i learned you were insane.
supporting fearmongering leaders and
believing deranged conspiracies.
i should have stopped with you then,
should have blocked you,
should have signed you up
for spam e-mail lists
about reverse mortgages
and hair replacement treatments,
but i tried to reason with you,
to change your mind.
i could not reconcile
i felt so connected
to someone so awful.

where does love lead us anyway?

<u>acting</u>

one of my acting teachers
after every performance
would ask
is this a love scene,
or a power scene?
and because i am a writer
before i am an actor
i usually got that question right.

in one class
i was assigned the final scene from
An Affair To Remember.
my teacher barely let me
get through the door
and start talking to terry
before she stopped me
and made me start all over.
again and again
she had me start from the top.
it did not look like
my nickie loved terry
as soon as he saw her.

on the fourth or fifth
or fiftieth try
my teacher,
exasperated,
yelled out,

caleb!
have you ever
been in love?!

without a second thought,
without even checking
in with myself,
i fired back,
nope!
and walked back
to the door to start again.

the many characters
that i take on.

<u>texting</u>

i watch the
text messages roll in

wyd
about to eat dinner.
i'm in love with you lol
why is that funny?
can you send me something?
send you what?
you know what
with suggestive eyes emoji.
oh.

people are exhausting.
why do we speak
in acronyms now?
or snap and chat
our way through
online acquaintances
based entirely on sex?

the internet has
distorted,
eroded,
ruined
romance.
back to the woods
to hunt for deafening quiet.

<u>turn around</u>

just a one-time thing.
bored friday night,
and then you would disappear.
but when i open the door
your golden brown eyes
steal my breath.

you're really hot
i blurt out.
with a devilish grin,
your eyes never leaving mine
you say,
you are too.
i do not even care
if you are just being polite.

later,
you start to leave
and i feel a wave of sadness,
not wanting you to go.
missing you already.
any feelings at all
for such a brief encounter
leave me embarrassed.
so i hold my tongue,
and pride,
and walk you
down the hall.

this will pass.
the hallway is ending.
it always does.

your hand is on the door.

but before you walk out
and begin the half-life
of your decaying memory
you turn around.
your burning eyes
find me,
grab me,
threaten to burn me
from the inside out.
my feet melt into the floor.

without a word,
without a breath,
you close the distance between us.
and you kiss me
like you mean it.

first sight

the ones who make you forget
what sleep even is,
let alone allow you to fall into it.

staring at the ceiling
for hours into pitch black,
trying to pick out
individual ceiling fan blades
spinning in a single blurred shadow.
repeating images of
your eyes dancing over my bare skin,
your fingertips sliding across my chest.
i stretch my hand into the darkness,
feeling for your phantom,
the smooth slopes down your back.
those full, firm lips.

closing my eyes,
going back farther,
opening the door again,
seeing you for the first time.
our eyes drawn together
like magnets that had
repelled all else until then,
so they dare not look away,
not when they have found
a bond like this.

i saw universes
in those golden orbs
that you used to entrap me.

for the first time,
i believed them all.
love at first sight
is real.

learning something new

the ache i never expected.
the longing.
i do not know if this is love,
or just some unending sensation
that blends lust, yearning,
and desperation
all in one smoky jar.

i do know that i want you back.
here in my bed
in my arms
the lights out
the power gone
the air still
the world on mute
so i can hear every breath
that leaves your lips.

you slipping your fingers
in between mine,
gripping me,
holding on to me,
because you cannot bear
to let me go either,
the most wanted
and needed
i have ever felt.

how have i never lived this before?
my only chance at survival
is to drown myself in you
again and again and again.

<u>fighting with indifference</u>

arguing with you
is like battling
a perpetually affirming shrink.
a lot of me talking
and a lot of you responding
okay.
i get that.
and my personal
favorite
you have a right
to feel that way
as if my permission
was ever in question.

there is no
lover's quarrel.
no real argument.
and certainly no growth
or understanding.
you swallow
my grievances
to feed the abyss
in your chest.

<u>wedding bells</u>

i have thought about my wedding
from time to time.
not the details.
not the tablecloth colors
or the flowers
or the menu.
but i have thought about it.
where it might happen,
who will be there,
but i suppose most of all,
how it will feel.
it has almost always
been an abstract thing.
indefinite enough
to never see who
stands next to me.

an early thursday dinner,
fajitas and strong margaritas.
you tell me,
suddenly and unprompted,
that you imagined what
our wedding would look like.
you don't have all of the
details down,
but you share what you know
smiling the smile
that i now know
is your real one,
the one burned behind
my eyes forever.
you speak of sleek white chairs,

a small crowd,
everyone outside,
and me in a givenchy suit.
you know i will
want to look good.

now i can hardly stop myself
from painting into open air
the rest of the scene,
building a world
off your foundation.

for years,
it is still the most vivid
wedding in my mind.

happy birthday

sitting in a pretentious bar
on my birthday.
overpriced drinks
with silly names
but my friends keep
buying them for me.
i smile through sips
and playful jokes at my expense,
stealing glances at my phone
to see if you have said anything,
it is my birthday after all.

i drift away,
allowing myself to imagine
a better story.
one where instead of
you forgetting my birthday,
i look up mid-laughter,
maybe carelessly spilling
a bit of my drink,
and just like a movie,
i see you across the room,
suddenly here,
out of nowhere,
looking so damn amazing,
smiling and looking at me
like i am the only one here,
and everything fades away,
the friends, the music, the drinks,
and i only see you.

but instead,
you never even send a text.
so i sit at this table,
well after midnight,
barely paying attention
to friends who care enough
to take me out on my birthday.
i am too sad
that you cannot be bothered,
and too mad
that i cannot give you up.

friday nights

another week has departed,
ushering in the forty-eight hour break
before dread creeps back in,
infiltrating your gut,
your chest,
your whole body,
your sofa,
your entire living room,
your sink of dirty dishes.

but i spend most of these
friday nights alone.
i check my phone
every three minutes,
and sometimes there is a message,
and sometimes there is not,
but it is never you anyway,
so i get frustrated with friends
for taking up digital space
that you never intended to fill.

i pour a glass of wine,
i decide to take a bath.
i take two sips and forget
where i set the glass down.
i feel too hot
so i unplug the tub
and watch the water disappear.
the liquid leaves so slowly.
it wants to give me a second chance,
there is still time to make something
of this night that demands the

celebration of freedom.
i may not be at a dark, loud bar
holding a glass i downed too quickly,
but i can still have a bath
and live a little.

i swing my bare feet over the ledge,
expecting a tingling warmth,
but my toes land on a dry bottom.
the clock on the counter says
it is past midnight.

just friends

never date a friend
never date a friend

for fucks sake,
remember it this time.

never date a friend.

swimming back

like salmon finding
their way home from
an exhausting year,
we always know our way back
to those who hurt us first,
those who hurt us worst.

you and me,
back in our old haunts.
ghosts walk between us
no matter where we go.

sitting in your car
i close my eyes
and tell you i want to say something
and you tell me to say it
and i tell you i will feel stupid
and you tell me to say it
and i tell you i don't want to
and you tell me to say it

and i say i love you
and you say you love me too.

the parking lot with
buzzing lanterns
and busted concrete blocks
all disappear.
i only need the light
in your eyes anyway.

i kiss you
and forget all of the bad
from an hour ago,
from a week ago,
from a year ago.
i have found my way back
to what i wish was home.

mirror image

one week after
i said i love you
in one parking lot,
i call you from
a different one.
i haven't even ever been
inside this coffee shop.
someone told me it is
a good writing spot.
so far,
i think it has a nice parking lot.
plenty of spaces wide enough
for me to think.

the voice memo i send you
asks why nothing changed
after the things we said.
why it is all exactly
how it was before i said,
we both said,
i love you.

nothing changed.

i back up and leave
the coffee shop
without ever going inside,
dreading the thought of caffeine
keeping me awake
even one more second.

<u>waiting game</u>

waiting for someone
to become who you
want them to be
is a game that will
far outlast the sun.
but for you,
for so long,
i was willing to test my endurance,
glaring at that taunting golden orb,
always putting the spotlight
on my hands,
the ones you haven't held in weeks,
on my lips,
the ones cracked and split
while i waited for you
to press your life back into them.

then i came to understand
that just as with the sun,
i must block from you
what is mine and most exposed
to keep from getting burned.

i told you i was moving to los angeles.
you said i should wait for you.

i drove west so fast
to chase the setting sun.

<u>the chase</u>

a thousand bee stings
in my stomach,
a constant chill
along my skin.
numb fingers,
heavy feet.
an ever-dwindling appetite.
a sensitivity to being awake.

and yet,
even with this
sickly slice
of my former self
that remains after you
had your feast...

i cannot forget
what love can feel like.
i will still chase it.
i will find it in a form
that lasts.

V.

starting over

i have been in this
new sunny city
for many months.
but it was not until now
that i feel it to be completely
fresh and new.
two things i left behind:
the love that will never work
and the relationship
that had no love in it.

how will i meet
someone new here?
should i?
it is still a pandemic after all,
if you are one of those,
like me,
who believes in science.

there are so many
people here.
walking the beach,
hiking the hills,
and writing poetry
at local artsy coffee shops,
never quite finishing
their iced oat milk lattes.

how old will i be
when i can finally
stop starting over?

film

if love is hard and
too much work,
then we should call that
something else.
love should be the thing
i escape to.
a door always open
but only accessible to me,
never admitting the
troubles that nest
up and down my skin.
they must wait outside.

in this new home,
i seek refuge at the new beverly cinema.
there is love in the journey even.
leaving my apartment
and cell phone behind.
walking la brea avenue,
the hills on my shoulder
the whole way there.
last minute tickets at the window.
a film shown *on film*,
one i have seen many times before,
but in these foldout fabric chairs,
sitting alone with a popcorn bucket,
i am wrapped in a butter-scented cocoon,
and my universe does not reach
beyond this small theater.

i eat every single kernel.
i read every single rolling credit

and am the last one to leave.
it is june,
but when i step outside
to the summer night,
i regret that i have no coat.

<u>it's early</u>

brunch,
and it's loud.
plates clanking,
people shouting,
and pop music
that i do not even like.

our waitress
is inattentive.
you order the
standard american platter.
when it comes to breakfast,
you like things simple,
you tell me.
a basic admission,
but it feels so personal.
maybe it's your easy smile
and confidence.
i have anxiously downed
half my coffee,
burning my tongue
in the process.
but you seem calm.
settled.
stable.

you feel like something
i can hold on to.

<u>december</u>

december seems like
too perfect of a time
to fall for someone.
the air is cold,
but the world is warm,
kindled by holiday lights
and fuzzy feelings
from the same movies
that play every year.
those films are the only way
i have experienced winter romance.

i have been dumped
in december at least once,
maybe twice if i think back hard enough,
which i would rather not do
because i am driving through
the countryside,
four hours on roads
i have never seen
to be with you.

this feels terrifying.
this feels exciting.

<u>stars</u>

years have passed
since i stayed up late
and talked with the stars.
my back flat against the driveway
outside my childhood home,
conversing with the cosmos
through words or some other way,
staring for hours at that twinkling sky.
i don't know if it was me
or those stars
who stopped coming out first.
but at some point,
the millions of light years
made our talks too strained.

but now i think of you,
still so new to me,
and i can barely catch my breath.
no one on this planet will understand.
i fear judgment
and questions i do not care to answer,
so i long for those constellation counselors
who heard my youthful dreams in detail,
and only shined brighter as the night aged.

i drive for miles and miles
to leave crisscrossing highways behind
and find a field whose
only neighbors are mountains.
the stars welcome me back
and ask how i have been,
but i tell them the past is unimportant

because the only story worth telling
is this new one with you,
and i tell them the tale
so that they will honor it
with bright light forever.

history

we learned plenty
of texas history growing up.
but in this boutique hotel
i have forgotten all these names
that are written on different doors.
i just know one of them
is for me and you.

heavy drapes
thin walls
good air conditioning
a firm bed.

you take a nap.
it is the first time i see you sleep.
you seem so innocent
and untroubled,
making me curious
if the first is true
and jealous
that you have found
a path to the second.

i take a photo,
hoping to make you laugh
when you wake up,
but later i forget.

midnight nears.
the bedside lamp glowing orange
is the only light on our bare bodies.
i guess the gummies

were stronger than i thought.
i quickly lose my sense
of where you and i
and the thick white sheets
all end and begin.
we float from mattress to ceiling
and sometimes hang suspended
in between,
but my fingers never lose yours.
my skin carries a current,
at any moment i may be shocked
out of my own body.

my eyes find yours
and the rhythm slows.
the air has fled the room
and there is only enough
oxygen for us to share a breath.
our bodies inhale and release
in historic harmony.
they may need to rename this room.

i almost say it then,
that i love you,
i love you i love you i love you.

never stop looking at me.

<u>open eyes</u>

the beautiful things you miss
when your head is down
for years at a time.

dogs smiling.
an empty street at sunset.
how we all walk differently
in the rain.
a pair of birds dancing under the sun,
hopping from pavement
to wooden post
to tree branch
then taking flight,
finding a new residential block
to see if earth reveals herself differently.

watching the cashier's face light up
when i say *thank you, have a great day*,
because i am finally living
with enough joy to mean it.

you pulled me out of
a dim, narrowing tunnel,
and now i choose to smile.
i do not avoid eye contact
with passerby.
i buy ice cream on the way home,
sometimes two scoops.

and i find you so many places.
your name on my phone.
the card you sent

sitting on my desk.
coffee every morning
thinking how strange it is
that you do not like it.
the song playing with the lyrics
you texted me the first night we met.
you are always nearby.
the rest of the world
is reborn to me in colors
that require new names.

i hate the internet

should i change
for the sake of love?
for someone else?
crowds comprised of friends
and those who always
have something to say
flood me with reminders
backed by internet memes
that *you are good enough*
and *change for no one.*

but i want to grow
with someone.
learn.
improve.
find the right key
to strike into symbiotic song
with a kindred soul.
i cannot feed and be fed
without change.
the trees change at least
every couple of miles,
and so do the paths
that start out straight,
so i must too
if i am to keep pace
with the one walking with me.

but how do you know
when the change is good?
and when it is
something else?

there are too many shadows
in these woods,
and sometimes mine
stares back at me
as i walk by.

mornings

i wake up every morning
in love.
i do not know
if this is a distinct feeling,
this *morning in love*,
or if it is just that
i am in love,
and it is morning.

i just know that when i wake up,
before the sun can slip
through cracks in the curtains,
my eyes open,
and even blurry with sleep
and burdened with bad vision
i see your outline next to me.
while the world still
slumbers around us
i pull myself closer
to feel you against me
simply because i must.
i hold on to you,
hoping the bliss that comes
before the day warms
fuses with my bones forever.
these are good mornings.

<u>so many things</u>

you do not like coffee
and i wonder if
you are even a human.

you wake easier than me.
or i am just slower
to leave bed now
with you in it.

you love to
ask the waitress
for her recommendation,
and you actually
trust her.

i suddenly have a list of things.
beaches or mountains and
thai food spice level and
ice cream flavors and
comfort movie.
i want to know them all,
but this steady discovery
is my favorite journey.

italian food

bad things happen
in places you love.
cracks climb the walls
that you will see every time
you return.

it is one of my favorite
italian restaurants
and no one could
tarnish the place like you.

why did you have to say that?
you know i am sensitive about it.
did you mean to hurt me?
you know how i can shut down.

i barely speak the rest of dinner.
hardly eat the pasta in front of me,
even with the truffle
filling the cold air between us.
we walk back to my car
and i conspire to not speak to you
for the rest of the night.
i run through the inventory
of things i need in my house:
noise-canceling headphones,
a pillow to sleep on the couch,
an unopened bag of
reese's peanut butter cups.

on the silent drive home
you reach for my hand.

i squeeze it without looking.
there are many other
italian restaurants in this city.

research

i am learning
all of your laughs.

the light snicker.
you are amused but
do not want to be the one
to break up the conversation.

the practiced *huh-huh-huh*.
you are on a video conference work call
and your acting is superb.

the quiet chuckle.
you find something funny.
truly funny.
your eyes begin to close,
your head tilts down,
and you try to hold
your glee inside
so that you are not too loud.

the one i love the most.
your eyes widen,
your mouth opens,
both lost to your control.
laughs come in short, rapid breaths,
each one chasing the last
into the open air.

i share this research with no one.
only i should hold the keys to this safe.

vacation

memorial day weekend getaway
and i wonder how
i will recall all of this
years from now.

we go to the mountains,
the place you love.
we go with your friends,
the people you love.
a trip with your chosen family
and i am scared.
the fewer the attachments,
the easier it is to break free.
and since we are celebrating history,
i have a long record
of rationing how connected
i allow myself to be
anytime i feel uncertain
which is every single time.

but you asked me to go with you.
and even though i was nervous,
even though i did not want to,
even though i could summon
a million excuses—
the joker i always keep
in my front pocket—
i said yes.

i watched you come alive
in those mountains.
some perfect potion of

cool morning air,
distant thunderous waterfalls,
and crunching along switchbacks
woke you in a way
i had not yet witnessed.

one,
we stand together
on an outlook more beautiful
than i could have imagined,
vast and wide and deep,
seemingly endless,
and i imagine the possibilities with you.

two,
we sit side by side
on a log at the water's edge
and i can tell this lake is cold
without ever dipping my feet
just like i can feel your lips form a smile
without even looking over.

three,
we see each other
across the dark firelit room
while laughing
at your friends debating,
and i wonder how fear
ever found me.

<u>spoken in the dark</u>

tonight is not even the end.
you still have one more week.
but the terror
of losing the weight of you,
of no longer waking up
to your hand around my arm,
your smile wide,
your eyes shut,
and your raspy *good morning*,
you always say good morning first,
of having no more easy conversations
because you are just one room away,
of walking any sidewalk again
without you a hand grab away,
forces me to rewrite all my rules of old.
i bury my inhibitions in a place
i will never find again.

i almost said it so many times before.
when you looked into my eyes
for a few seconds longer
and dared to pull every truth out of me.
or when i left to run some errand,
so quickly and casually,
giving you no time to react.
or when your bare body
lied beneath mine,
in a rush of euphoria,
when i would lose my mind
and grip on language
except for those three words.

still i have always stopped short,
clutching to some sense of safety.
but in one week's time,
you will leave me.
i honestly do not know
if it is more important for you to know
or for me to know that you know,
and maybe those are the
same thing anyway.

i wait until night,
feeling safer cloaked in dark.
your back turned to me,
i dig deep into my heart and soul
to find the bridge
now connecting them.

are you tired?
mmhmm.
are you falling asleep?
mmhmm.

i pause,
almost convince myself
to hold back
like every time before.
but then a rush of courage,
a more certain thump in my heart.

i love you.

at first, silence.
have you fallen asleep
from my slightest delay?

or is it the alternative,
too painful to bear?
but then you turn to me,
and with just more than a whisper,
soft and melodious
and certain,

i love you too Caleb.

and for one brief fleeting moment
one quick breath in the dark,
i feel whole.

<u>when you hold my hand</u>

work was bad for you today.
we walk to pick up
thai for dinner.
you need fresh air
and i always want thai food.

i only need a few blocks
to sense the stress
pulsing through you.
you're quiet.
tense.
walking faster than usual.

you suddenly grab my hand.
you don't look over at me,
but your fingers
lock into mine.
i give your hand
a squeeze
and i hold on tight.

i imagine
the moon growing and shrinking
in an endless cycle,
and all the while
my hand is the one
you always reach for.

<u>different</u>

every other time
hearing *i love you*
just felt nice.
from you,
it feels like a promise.

hot tea,
the trickling warmth
never leaves.
your favorite song,
on repeat the chorus
never grows dull.
endless mountains on the horizon,
not daunting—
an adventure under
big blue skies.

<u>work</u>

i may have to quit my job.
it steals time i should spend
falling onto my couch,
onto you,
your arms around me,
closing the space so tight
that subatomic particles
must scatter.

sometimes we are quiet.
sometimes you make me laugh
and my body lightly quakes
against yours.

surely this is how
i am to spend
my working hours
and all of the
other hours too.

<u>missing out</u>

as a child,
i missed out on traveling.
rarely leaving the state,
never the country.
sidelined from searching
for traces of the places
my books described to me
as far better than
my small adolescent world.
but that was a gap
i could comprehend
like any school exam.
it took time and work
and some course correction
but i solved the equation
and spent much of my twenties
crisscrossing the planet.

but nothing could prepare me
for this feeling.
an emotional peak
i have reached
believing you love me.
comfort and joy and more smiles
than i can remember,
but even those are not the surprise.
what makes me skip mirrors
and forget names
is a feeling i had never known,
not heard even a myth of,
the kind whispered from
town to town.

you loving me
made me love myself,
an intervention too divine
for my own earthly works
to dig up from the ground.

<u>afraid</u>

doubt never infects you
the same way twice.
even as the body adapts
to abrupt shifts in tone,
names you've never heard,
nights without a word,
infection can work its way
into a new corner of your mind.

did i admit love only because
i was afraid i might lose it?
did i surrender too much
and now you would rather not
play these records ever again?
so many scratches.
the sound is not quite
as melodious as before.
did i catch you only
in a moment,
one never to set in amber,
merely a footprint
that will vanish
with the first rain?

the sun grows weary from
keeping me in the light,
so it goes west with the waves.
if only we both could follow.
but you have no appetite
for my stories.
i swallow every last thought.
my fever rises.

VI.

<u>vindicated</u>

i confessed to you
that for most of my life
i have felt unlovable.

two weeks later
you told me we were over.

if there is
one thing i love,
it is being proven right.

left behind

you never lived here
but your things litter my house.
cards,
a hat,
a padres jersey
that i refuse to wear.

i want to burn them.

i want them to
never disappear.

my mind changes
as quickly as the weather.
sometimes i walk by
and pretend these things
are not there.
other times i cannot help
but imagine that you still are.
they are.
you are.
i can smell your shampoo
in every room.

at night,
i close my eyes as i get into bed,
not daring to look
at the space next to me.
i open them only to
safely stare into darkness,
up at the ceiling,
until i might burn a hole

and glimpse a path
to a different galaxy,
so that i might escape
the risk of turning
to the other side of the bed,
your side of the bed,
where i would lay eyes
on the specter
that will follow me
to my days as dust.

<u>tragedies</u>

shakespeare's editors
called the plays tragedies,
but people want to find
the good in them.

tragedies.
not all ends well.

i would have settled
for the role of comic relief
so that my story
did not become
a modern realization.
turn the spotlight
on someone stronger.
let me exit stage left
before the poison brews,
before the madness spews.

<u>beer cans in a bar</u>

one month after
my world crumbled.
i have put out the flames,
at least those i can see so far,
but smoke still swells
in my lungs
night and day.

against my better judgment,
and what should it matter
because what is there to
balance against anymore,
i see you again.

a golden hour walk
to bar food and beer cans.
even after weeks of
mentally journaling you
into a disfigured tyrant
who should be sent to a lab
so that the white coat brigade
can finally declare alien life exists,
sitting side by side in this bar
i am still drawn to you.
i want your head to explode,
but i want to sit here with you
until it happens.

i cannot let you know.
i cannot let you believe
that i am so desperate.
so i mime minimalism

and press record,
waiting for you to show me
that you still want me, too.
that you still feel the same.
mostly the same.
a little the same.
something.
anything.
my face paint is dripping,
it's the sweat
it's the july heat
it's condensation from the beer cans.
from that second beer can.
we are drinking beer cans
because the bar has
no beer on draught today.
no draught beer in a bar.
what a contradictory moment we are.

i try to make you laugh.
you do a few times.
they are not real.
i still remember
all of those laughs well.
you never make eye contact
for more than a second,
as if the month apart
has sent me to such dark places
that i returned to the surface
having grown glaring snakes
from the top of my head.

each sip,
each bite,

each forced few lines
make me want to
burn this place to the ground.
i would let everyone escape
except me.
instead i let you talk about
your awful boss
and the dumb things
she said this week.
my dutiful ear,
my fraudulent cheer.

<u>where are the doctors</u>

diagnosing love
is a fool's errand.
we chase after
and pine for
and dream of
something that is
sure to end.
the only uncertainty
are the details
that the devil deals us.
it may be true that
our bodies only die once
but wildflowers come
every spring,
unrequested.
and even though
you closed the door,
it still has a way of slamming
into my face at least
one more time.

wednesday

something new came
when i thought
nothing ever would.
even though i am still hurting,
even though i am deeply afraid,
i leave my cave,
still sure snow survives
even if it cannot be seen.

we talk over coffee.
i like that you like coffee.
it is nice to talk to someone
who likes coffee again
even if you use artificial sweetener.

a wednesday.
but i do not remember
much else of the world
around us.
the notes only say
that we sit for a long time,
conversation comes
like breathing,
i laugh more
than i have in months.

new things

watching sunset
with you in a park,
old to the city,
new to me.
tourists and loud children
and roaming dogs not on leashes,
all things that usually
make me want to go home.
but then you hand me a seltzer,
the kind of thing i never drink,
and ask me how my day was,
the kind of thing i do not expect,
and it is somehow still warm
up on this hill.

recounting my day
puts me on a slippery slope,
i have not done this in a while,
but now i am telling you
about drama with my family
a thousand miles away,
leaning on laughter
between sentences
just in case it is all too much.
but you tell me of your life,
and i listen without wondering
how we will eventually
stop talking to one another.
i see you and the
pink purple night sky
and another seltzer in my hand.

<u>sleeping</u>

i wake slowly,
my arms still around you.
i stay there, still,
cautious of the crime
of stirring your perfect form.
i lie back,
eyes wide,
inches between our bodies,
casting you into a fresco
they will not find for centuries.
i hope they find me there, too.

recalling the rush of
asking you to stay the night,
telling myself it is too soon,
if not for you
then definitely for me,
but you nodding
and smiling
and me breathing
and easing.

your shoulder leads
the rest of you, slowly,
up and down,
up and down.
i lose count
and time along with it.
you look so comfortable,
so at peace,
like maybe you are
supposed to be right here.

before the light enters
to cast us in new colors
i allow myself to believe it.

<u>twist</u>

you tricked me
by being a good
communicator.
you were the
broken one,
or at least the one
who owned up to it.
you asked me to always
be honest with you
about how i felt.
we talked like
emotionally mature adults
are supposed to.
i was sure i hit the jackpot.

but you were no different.
every court jester
has a spare robe
for a royal ruse.

you,
like everyone else before,
gifted me that same feeling
of overwhelming dread.
the violent storm
in my gut,
warning me that
i am hurtling toward
an end.
i always see the storm
but invariably believe
i am the one to weather it.

but i am no different.
every storm chaser
has a frayed coat
for a rainy run.

<u>upside</u>

at least
you helped me
get hotter.
i am now
in the best shape
of my life.
hotter than ever.
i mark a tally in
the win column.

ghost runner

this ghost that lives with me
is a runner.
i beg it to run outside
like a normal person,
like i do,
to give us both some space.
but it runs only in this house,
and i suspect only
when i am present,
always finding a path
just out of sight,
never sprinting,
moving at a comfortable pace
so that i can still see
the dust it kicks up,
still smell your hair,
still see the shine of your eyes,
still see the blur of your hand
as if i can still reach out and grab it.
but i will never be that fast.

<u>museum date</u>

i tell myself
i do not need another love.
but somehow,
i am on a date at the museum.
my date is nice.
friendly.
possibly attractive.
but i do not really
want to be here.
i feel the itch to check my phone
for notifications that
i will swipe away anyway.
i pretend to be interested
by exhibits i saw
two months ago
when i came alone
and enjoyed them.

in elementary school
i once thought about
pulling the emergency fire alarm
just because i did not feel
like being there that day.

i scour the room for red.

<u>and again</u>

another failed relationship.
i get over this one in four days.
but now i am pressed against
a familiar fog,
itching to whisper your name
so it will let me pass,
desperate to feel weight
at my side once more.

beyond that mist
there are gravestones
and broken benches.
but i do not need a seat,
i do not even need to stay long,
the air is cool enough
to dance for a while.
they will play vinyl records
because it must sound old,
but it will be charming.
some of the lyrics have changed,
but so have i,
so i tell myself it is fine,
i can sing this song still,
i can dance,
i can live in a forlorn garden,
black flowers are
still flowers after all.
but even in a place
as dark as this,
the ghost of you
never shows.

<u>hints</u>

a speakeasy
when it was still
cold outside.
telling you and telling myself,
that you are so nice.
i did so forgetting
principles of data
and the scientific method,
dealing in deep hope
and recalled book passages
that are a little fuzzy
just like me from this drink.

i should have taken a hint
when you said
nothing back.

all the times
i lied to myself
to see someone else.

judgment

these days
i walk with my head down.
i am too embarrassed
passerby will see
the pain in my eyes
that i swore i would
never meet.

what if they offer help?
eye me with concern?
feel sorry for the boy
who came from a humble start
but was blessed with a brain
and magnifying glass
to discern the world around him
and yet grew too curious,
too undisciplined,
turned his eye to the sun,
lost his way,
burned his wings,
and crashed to the earth?
or will they
simply scoff?

i cannot bear to learn
the answer.
so i walk with
a steady, simple,
unremarkable pace,
my head down
watching repeating cracks
in the sidewalk,

dreaming of star systems
that have heard
different stories.

december again

christmas eve
and i cannot sleep.

i think about the pillow
i gave you,
wondering if you kept it,
and if you did,
if you think of me
when you see it,
or if you sleep on it,
and lie sleepless too,
thinking on everything that happened,
rattling between the good times
and the pain,
like i do now.

i wonder if you regret it,
like i said you would
the last time i saw you.
but even in that moment
when i could hate you most,
i still hoped the regret
would not find you.
somehow, i still wanted
you to be happy.

now i do not.
now i hope you do regret it.
now i hope you cannot be
happy without me.
that is the only route to save myself,
the only way to stop myself

from screaming
into this dark room,
with not even the beauty
of a white christmas
to cheer me up
in december,
because it is hot and barren
in texas like usual
in december,
and i am awake and alone
in texas once again
in december.

<u>aftertaste</u>

is it not actually love,
again,
unless it makes me forget you?

will there ever be a time
when i do not have to persuade myself,
every day,
even the best days,
even summiting a mountain
under a pure blue sky,
even snuggled close on the couch and
more interested in the gaps
between fingers
than whatever plays on screen,
that yes *this* can be love,
that i am already starting
to think that it is,
that the electric current
coursing through me
with every touch
is the proof?

will you ever just
slip away,
so i can remember
everything that can fill a sky?
or will that single word
always taste of you
as i breathe it out,
even if just a whisper?

VII.

the portrait

i want the version of you
i know does not exist.
it never did.

i tattooed new patterns
all over you as i slept
those many months,
filling gaps and
covering stains.
the going was slow
as art always is,
so i hid my work
even from myself.

but now the trick
of your painting is exposed.
my amaranths and aquas,
my aureolins and amethysts
all twist and crack
to colors we do not name
other than something gray,
the form of you we
had all been hiding from.

yet the lost painting
still lives in my mind.
i must steer clear
of every blank canvas
and any white wall.
my hands are dangerous
when idle for too long,
itching to return to work.

old ways

i have returned
to my old ways.
empty weekends,
baking out of the box,
and candles.

i am back at the cinema
on weeknights alone.
it is nice to go
to the movies again,
eating popcorn buckets
to the bare bottom.

i run with the sunrise
and wonder
why i ever stopped.
i go to bed later,
charged on late night tea
and novels that for months
laid in wait all over the house
for the day they might be chosen.

and this feels fine,
to be back where i guess
i belong.
a time to test
just how much comfort
comes with familiarity.

<u>swim</u>

a text message
from the first one
i looked at in the eyes and said
i love you
and knew what that meant.
the owls must have been busy
because this comes
after half a year of silence.

i usually still bite and
allow you to drag me
through the motions.
smiling
and laughing
and reminiscing
and getting anxious
and not sleeping
and double, triple texting back
and feeling that same unbearable emptiness
in my stomach that consumes
every piece of me.

this time though,
i suppress my appetite.
your bait can linger
for another.
i swim downstream
for miles and miles.

<u>tuesday</u>

i have been kissing
someone new for two weeks now.
we watch a movie together,
curled up on the couch.
it feels oddly comfortable.

i could be sprinting ahead,
imagining three months later
and knowing each other's friends,
eight months and
no longer vacationing alone.
but my thoughts leave the path,
straying far from it.
i slip into mud that pulls me
under slowly and deliberately,
so i have time to feel every
single inch of the descent.
the couch with smooth fingers
and tangled feet
is now light years away.
i imagine how i will recall
this memory from the other side,
when the couch is empty
but for a new imprint
now joining the others.

i pull back my fingers and feet
you leave before the movie ends.
we are both tired.
it is a tuesday anyway.
i never hear the front door close.

<u>code breaker</u>

you have rewired me.
turned me into
a code breaker.
i read signs
all the time,
even if they are
not there.
i keep a journal
with me always,
heavy with entries,
inked in many colors,
rarely dated
but always fresh.
i reference it with every step.
i walk away long before
i can even smell the wet wood
of the plank that dangles
above the choppy sea.

loving this city

renewing my vows
with the city of angels,
a love affair i can
tend to every day.

i did not make it here
until my thirties
so maybe it was easier
to fall in love with her
and not burn through
that romance on the end
of a match.

every saturday is a
different donut shop,
sundays are for bagels.
i meet the morning by
running the sands of santa monica,
down through venice where vendors
start to set up shop,
and as i turn back
some give me a wave,
they must recognize me now
as part of whatever
we are all doing here.

for me, i am never
too sure anymore.
i write a little here,
i try a new restaurant,
i delete an entire draft,
i walk to a new park

so i can see how it reveals itself.
i love june gloom
until i do not.
i love the july sun,
until i long for colder days
that may not arrive
until november.
a new story unravels
every day in this city
as long as i get out of bed
to go looking for it,
and some days i try.

<u>just go</u>

give up on romance,
loving your friends is enough,
you tell yourself.
they are the ones there
for coffee
for long night drives
for screaming your favorite song
for reading your face before you have to say it
for listening.

the love you need.
they never leave.

until they do.
until the one who
you were so sure about
shows up in a new mask.
you ask about it,
the oversaturated color
and irregular shape.
but they push away
those accusations,
ghosting by day,
gaslighting by night
until the mask gives you
such bad motion sickness
that you must step off
and leave.

back to the trees
and streams that run cold
you go.

<u>know</u>

you can tell your friends
all your want about me.
sip cheap wine
over shared screens
as you all laugh
at a version of me
locked in a bedside chest,
a token to remind you,
to convince you,
that you did right.
go on,
make a cheers
to my downfall.
but you will always know
that i was the one next to you
when you spoke to the darkness
and laid bare your soul.

<u>other things</u>

i will search for other things.

a best friend
who can be a partner.

a winning combination
to game the genetic lottery
for a gold star child.

a wealthy divorcee
i meet in an overpriced hotel bar,
i will give good sex,
i will get a g wagon.

i will find none of it.
i will learn the ocean floor
and taste new languages.
i will debate my clone
and dance among the stars.
i will run farther.

<u>the flood</u>

every time
i almost call you,
text you,
send you a funny video—
every time
i start to almost hope
that there might be
one more chance—
i go back to that night,
rain slapping my windshield,
but i never heard it.
as i broke down,
i was deaf to the rest
of the natural world.
my body shook and shuddered,
and it was silent too,
quieter than the wind,
but far more weathered.
i told you how i felt.
wasted and meaningless.
used.
even though i deserved
to be chosen,
to be fought for,
to be wanted,
that sometimes i could not breathe
because i was sure,
so sure,
that you were the love of my life.

i knew what it meant
to say that now

and mean it.

then it was your turn
at silence.
you sat like a midwinter tree.
no leaves to even whisper.
no birds about you to sing.
you were frozen,
grim,
bare.

i unraveled,
revealing the despair
i had until then
kept guarded even from myself.

and you did nothing
and you said nothing
until you said you had to go.
so you got out,
and walked away,
unbothered by the pouring rain,
untroubled by anything.
you left me in my car
where i hoped the rain
would now fall biblically,
flooding everything in sight,
carrying me away
to never feel anything
ever
ever
again.

when i think of you,
and the thoughts
become too enticing,
i go back to that night.
i flee before i can
smell the rain.
my days as a storm chaser
are finished.

VIII.

<u>real</u>

knowing love is different
for everyone.
worrying i had a shot
at the real thing,
the *really real* thing,
and i lost it.
it felt good
and real
and special
and surprising
and everything i wanted
and it vanished.
searching for scents of life
i used to tell myself
were far greater
than the fruitless labor
of looking for love.

move on

love and me
have been dancing
a long time now.
i have gone through many stages:
intrigued,
opposed,
apathetic,
experimental,
bored,
confident,
ruined.

i have looked through
magnifying glasses of different designs,
twisted and turned
my head to alter the angle of my view,
slept on it,
prayed for it,
talked through it,
wrote about it,
and think maybe it is
finally time to drop
this pail of water
with so many holes
and walk away from
this burning house.

<u>change</u>

or maybe we are only doomed
until we are not.

perhaps this is not perpetual ruin,
but a carousel that knows
only a breakneck speed,
spinning endlessly
and furiously,
on it we move about,
sometimes carefully,
other times recklessly,
trying to reset our position,
the same ride but
from a new point of view,
but every change coming
with a new bruise,
until an exit simply
presents itself.

then, i should view each spin,
each failed love,
each mistake,
each heartbreak,
each defeat
as a chance to realize and learn
something about myself.
so that i am not surprised
when someone new
wants to give me a chance.

if the leaves can change,
then so can i.

Acknowledgments

Thank you to Caitlin Swedroe, Vadim Egoul, Samantha Brown, Lise Schwartzkopf, and Rachel Matovich for reading these poems before I was ready to share with anyone else.

Thank you to my friends for being unpaid therapists through many of the moments that inspired these poems.

And thank you for reading these poems now.

About The Author

Caleb Graves is a writer, director, screenwriter, and producer. He grew up in Stephenville, Texas, a small, rural town a couple of hours outside of Dallas. In his spare time, Caleb likes to run, travel, and eat donuts. Caleb now lives in southern California.

Made in United States
Troutdale, OR
09/20/2024